NBA FINALS

GLOBAL CITIZENS: SPORTS

Published in the United States of America by Cherry Lake Publishing
Ann Arbor, Michigan
www.cherrylakepublishing.com

Content Adviser: Liv Williams, Editor, www.iLivExtreme.com
Reading Adviser: Marla Conn, MS, Ed., Literacy specialist, Read-Ability, Inc.

Photo Credits: ©Brocreative/Shutterstock, cover, 1; ©Everett Historical/Shutterstock, 5; ©JoulyC/Shutterstock, 6; ©Jerry Coli/Dreamstime, 7, 19; ©Vera Iarochkina/Dreamstime, 8; ©John Christian Fjellestad/Shutterstock, 11; ©zhangjin_net/Shutterstock, 13; ©Alex Kravtsov/Shutterstock, 14; ©Noamfein/Dreamstime, 17; ©Martin Ellis/Dreamstime, 20; ©Blackkango/Dreamstime, 21; ©Wei Chuan Liu/Dreamstime, 22; ©Rawpixel.com/Shutterstock, 25; ©Eric Broder Van Dyke/Dreamstime, 26; ©Benkrut/Dreamstime, 28

Library of Congress Cataloging-in-Publication Data

Names: Hellebuyck, Adam, author. | Deimel, Laura, author.
Title: NBA Finals / written by Adam Hellebuyck and Laura Deimel.
Description: Ann Arbor, Michigan : Cherry Lake Publishing, [2019] | Series: Global Citizens: Sports | Audience: Grades 4 to 6 | Includes bibliographical references and index.
Identifiers: LCCN 2019004184 | ISBN 9781534147485 (hardcover) | ISBN 9781534150348 (paperback) | ISBN 9781534148918 (pdf) | ISBN 9781534151772 (hosted ebook)
Subjects: LCSH: NBA Finals (Basketball)—Juvenile literature. | National Basketball Association—Juvenile literature. | Basketball—Tournaments—United States—Juvenile literature.
Classification: LCC GV885.515.N37 H45 2019 | DDC 796.323/640973—dc23
LC record available at https://lccn.loc.gov/2019004184

Cherry Lake Publishing would like to acknowledge the work of the Partnership for 21st Century Learning. Please visit www.p21.org for more information.

Printed in the United States of America
Corporate Graphics

ABOUT THE AUTHORS

Laura Deimel is a fourth grade teacher and Adam Hellebuyck is a high school social studies teacher at University Liggett School in Grosse Pointe Woods, Michigan. They have worked together for the past 8 years and are thrilled they could combine two of their passions, reading and sports, into this work.

TABLE OF CONTENTS

CHAPTER 1

History: NBA Finals

Which basketball team is the best in North America? The National Basketball Association (NBA) figures this out every year by holding a tournament with the top 16 teams in the **league**. The best teams from the Eastern and Western **Conferences** are invited to compete against each other to determine the NBA champion for the year. The ultimate set of games between the two conference champions is called the NBA Finals.

The NBA used to be called the Basketball Association of America (BBA) until 1949.

In 1947, the Philadelphia Warriors beat the Chicago Stags by four games. The Chicago Stags only won one game.

How the NBA Finals Began

The first NBA Finals were held in 1947. That year, there were only 11 teams in the league. The Philadelphia Warriors defeated the Chicago Stags in the first championship. Since then, the number of teams involved in the NBA has changed greatly. The NBA has had as few as eight teams in the league and as many as 30. What started as a simple playoff has turned into one of the world's most watched sporting events!

[21ST CENTURY SKILLS LIBRARY]

From 1959 to 1966, the Boston Celtics won the NBA Finals 8 years in a row.

The Larry O'Brian NBA Championship Trophy is about 2 feet (0.6 meters) tall and weighs about 16 pounds (7.2 kilograms).

Man Behind the Trophy

The trophy that the championship team wins at the end of the NBA Finals is named after Larry O'Brien. O'Brien was the **commissioner** of the NBA from 1975 to 1984. He also served as the postmaster general of the United States. The postmaster general is in charge of making sure the mail is delivered around the country.

The Women's NBA Finals

In 1996, the NBA created the Women's National Basketball Association (WNBA) so women could also play professional basketball. There are currently 12 teams in the WNBA. Since the WNBA doesn't have as many teams as the NBA, the organization doesn't separate teams based on the conference they're in. Also, unlike the NBA Finals, the WNBA Finals invites the top eight teams in the league to play for the championship.

Developing Questions

*Throughout the history of the NBA Finals, some teams have won more than one, two, or even three championships! Many people label a team a **dynasty** when it wins a number of NBA Finals frequently over a short period of time. People often disagree on which NBA teams should be considered one. They might be using different ways of measuring what makes a team a dynasty. What questions would you ask when thinking about whether a certain NBA team is a dynasty team? Discuss these with a friend.*

CHAPTER 2

Geography: NBA Goes Global

While modern basketball was invented in the United States, it has been played around the world for decades. Recently, the NBA has started to gain international popularity. At each game of the Finals, 265 journalists from 35 different countries cover the action! The NBA Finals are now watched by an international audience. Not only that, but players from around the world are looking for ways to join the league!

The NBA organizes Basketball Without Borders, a program that brings the love of the game to young athletes in impoverished areas nationally and around the world.

China

Basketball has been one of the most popular sports in China since the 1930s. According to a survey, around 12.2 million people in China watched each game of the 2017 Finals on a digital device. Chinese **commentators** gave play-by-play reports of the action. Instead of reading translations of American commentators, people in China were able to follow the big game in their native language.

China has had six players participate in the NBA. The most famous was Yao Ming, who played for the Houston Rockets from 2002 to 2011. While Yao never made it to the NBA Finals, his success in the NBA brought even more Chinese interest to the league.

Most Represented Countries Outside of the United States in the NBA*

Country	Number of Players
Canada	11
Australia	9
France	9
Spain	7
Germany	6
Croatia	5
Serbia	5
Turkey	5

*As of the 2018–2019 season

The NBA account on Weibo (China's version of Twitter) had about 2.9 billion video views during the 2017 playoffs!

Experts believe that by 2025, about 1 in 7 people across the globe, or 1 billion people, will have some access to the NBA Finals.

Japan

Japan has had a long history with the NBA. The NBA played its first game outside of North America during the 1990 regular season, in Tokyo, Japan. In 2017, the NBA signed a deal with Rakuten, a Japanese technology company, to show games during the regular season and the NBA Finals to its 900 million users. The NBA will make around $225 million as a result of this agreement. The NBA is looking to build on this relationship to get even more people in Japan to watch the NBA Finals each year.

International Players in the NBA

Even though the NBA teams are all located in the United States (except for the Toronto Raptors, who are in Canada), not all players in the league are U.S. citizens. When players were being selected for the 2018–2019 **rosters**, there were 108 players from 42 countries and territories waiting to join a team.

Gathering and Evaluating Sources

Currently, the Dallas Mavericks have the most international players on their team—7 out of 17 total players. That is 41 percent of the team!

Imagine you are a player from another country who would like to play basketball in the NBA. What would your journey look like? How would you enter the United States? What steps would you need to take to work in the United States? What would an international player need to do to play in the NBA? Gather information from the internet and your local library. Read blogs, opinion pieces, and analytical articles on the topic of immigration and working visas. What did you learn from the information you gathered?

CHAPTER 3

Civics: Rules and Community

Winning the NBA Finals is a goal for all teams in the league. In order to keep the games fair, the NBA has many important rules to follow when qualifying for the tournament. Winning the NBA Finals is important not only to the teams, but also to the cities that host the Finals!

Important Rules for the NBA Finals

The NBA organizes its championship tournament very carefully. The NBA has divided teams into two conferences based on the teams' geographic locations: the Eastern Conference and the Western Conference. Both of these are divided into three divisions.

Despite the air conditioning failing and the temperature rising above 90° Fahrenheit (32° Celsius) during Game 1 of the 2014 NBA Finals, the game kept going!

Teams are ranked in their division and conference based on the number of games they have won. The top teams in each division and conference are then invited to enter the NBA Finals tournament. Teams from the Western Conference play each other in the tournament to determine the best team in that half of the league. The Eastern Conference teams do the same. The winner of the Western Conference then plays the winner of the Eastern Conference in a series of seven games to determine the NBA Finals champion.

Taking Informed Action

One reason NBA teams are divided into conferences and divisions is because of time zones. The **continental** United States has four different time zones: Eastern, Central, Mountain, and Pacific. If it is 9:00 p.m. in New York, which is in the Eastern time zone, it is 6:00 p.m. in Los Angeles, which is in the Pacific time zone. If the Los Angeles Clippers were playing the New York Knicks in New York at 8:00 p.m., people watching on television in Los Angeles would have to tune in live at 5:00 p.m.! It's easier on everyone if teams play other teams in their own time zone and geographic location.

Since 1955, the NBA gives a top player the NBA Finals
Most Valuable Player award.

The youngest player to play in the Finals and win a Championship was Darko Miličić from Serbia in 2004. He was 18 years old.

Although not the tallest player in NBA history, at 7 feet 5 inches (2.26 meters) Chuck Nevitt from Colorado is the tallest player to have played in the NBA Finals.

Community Pride

A community is very proud when its local team wins the NBA Finals. Cities will often hold a victory parade to honor their team. After the 2018 NBA Finals, hundreds of thousands of people lined the parade route in Oakland, California. People were honoring the Golden State Warriors' championship, wearing the team colors and holding signs with positive messages. The city of Oakland worked with the Golden State Warriors to plan the parade and make sure it would be both safe and fun for all the fans and players who

The top three teams that have won the most Championship titles are the Celtics, with 17; the Lakers, with 16; and the Bulls, with 6.

attended it. Many fans were inspired by Golden State's victory. One fan, who also plays basketball for his school, said that Stephen Curry's ability to shoot "threes" made him want to make more three-point shots in his games.

Teams that win the NBA Finals show their own pride in other ways. In addition to having a parade, the Detroit Pistons took the Larry O'Brien Championship Trophy on a tour of the entire state after winning the NBA Finals in 2004. This was the first time the trophy had traveled around the winning team's home state in the history of the NBA.

Developing Claims and Using Evidence

The NBA Finals are held in the cities of the two teams playing for the championship. The first two games are hosted by the team with "home court advantage." Home court advantage goes to the team that won more basketball games during the regular season. Teams like playing their games at home because they know the court better and their fans help to cheer them on. The next two games of the Finals are held in the other team's city. The rest of the games alternate between cities. Some people want to change this system to host all of the games in a neutral city. A neutral city is one that does not give a home court advantage to either team.

Do you think the current system needs to change? Why or why not? What would be the advantages and disadvantages of hosting the NBA Finals in a neutral city? What information would you need to make your decision? Use the evidence you find during your research to support your claim.

CHAPTER 4

Economics: Expensive Seats

The NBA is ranked third of all professional sports leagues in the amount of money it makes every year. The NBA Finals are a big part of why the league makes so much money. Let's find out how exactly this happens.

Sold-Out Tickets

The NBA Finals are so popular that tickets to the games usually sell out! The prices of these tickets aren't cheap, either. A ticket to game 1 of the 2018 Finals was $460! The average **resale price** for that ticket was $1,036.

The NBA has over 27.7 million followers on Twitter!

Sponsors

Because not everyone can **afford** to **watch** the game in **person**, most people watch from the comfort of their own homes. According to research, about 17.7 million people in the United States watched the 2018 NBA Finals! Companies that want to sell their products to viewers will often buy a commercial airtime slot during the game.

It is estimated that the Warriors were awarded a little over $3.3 million for winning the 2018 NBA Finals.

This is often referred to as sponsoring. These sponsors will show a commercial for their product to the millions of people watching the game. During the 2018 Finals, the average cost for a company to air a commercial was $500,000!

Salary Caps

In order to build a team that can win enough games to make it to the NBA Finals, coaches and team owners must think about economics. Each team is only allowed to spend a certain amount of money on players' **salaries**. This is called a team's salary cap. During the 2017–2018 season, the NBA's team salary cap was $99 million a year for each team.

Team owners, managers, and coaches have to think about how their team should spend the available money. Would they like to spend most of their salary cap to **acquire** one amazing basketball player? A good basketball player can sign a contract, or an agreement, to play the game for a large amount of money. Or would they rather spend the same amount of money to hire a few very talented players?

Taking Informed Action

Most professional sports leagues have a salary cap for each team. These salary caps try to keep each team competitive and also try to make sure that each player receives fair pay. Some people argue that there should not be a salary cap. They believe that teams should be able to pay players whatever they want. What do you think? Should the NBA keep its salary cap? What evidence do you have to support your answer?

You can share your opinion with the NBA online at https://contact.nba.com/contact-nba. Remember to use all of the tools you learned in your writing classes, like the traits of good writing, in your response!

According to a study, Cleveland, Ohio, saw an economic impact of about $3.7 million each day it hosted the 2018 NBA Finals.

Hosts

It's not just the teams and sponsors that benefit from the NBA Finals—the host cities do too! Because the games draw large crowds to the basketball arenas, there need to be more people working behind the scenes to ensure the games are enjoyed by all. This means more jobs—from selling tickets, food, and drinks to keeping the arena safe and secure. Shops and restaurants surrounding the arena also benefit. In fact, according to a survey, cities that host the NBA Finals saw on average a higher increase in employment compared to the national average that year.

Communicating Conclusions

The highest-paid player in the NBA during the 2017–2018 season was Golden State Warriors point guard Stephen Curry. He made $34.7 million during that season and signed a 5-year contract to make a total of $201.2 million! In contrast, WNBA players earn about $71,635 with a starting salary of $50,000 and a cap of $110,000. That's about 20 percent of what the lowest-paid NBA player makes. Why do you think there is a discrepancy in pay? Some say it's due to popularity—more people watch the NBA games than the WNBA games.

Talk to friends or family members who follow basketball. Ask them what they think about the salary gap. Is it fair? Why or why not?

Think About It

Examine the chart of NBA expansion from 1967 to today. What do you notice about the number of teams in the NBA? Why do you think some years had many more teams than others? Research what might have been happening in the United States and the world to affect the numbers. Think about how the different number of teams could impact the NBA Finals. Could this change the number of teams allowed to participate in the tournament?

NBA Expansion

Years	No. of Teams
1967–1968	12
1968–1970	14
1970–1974	17
1974–1976	18
1976–1980	22
1980–1988	23
1988–1989	25
1989–1995	27
1995–2004	29
2004–2019	30

For More Information

Further Reading

Doeden, Matt. *The NBA Playoffs: In Pursuit of Basketball Glory.* Minneapolis, MN: Millbrook Press, 2019.

Mortensen, Lori. *Maya Moore: Basketball Star.* North Mankato, MN: Snap Books, 2018.

Websites

NBA—Encyclopedia Playoff Edition: Greatest Final Performances
http://www.nba.com/history/finals/greatest_finals_performances.html
Read about the top 25 player performances in the history of the NBA Finals.

Sports Illustrated—Kids
https://www.sikids.com
Find in-depth articles about the WNBA and NBA at this site!

GLOSSARY

acquire (uh-KWIRE) to get

commentators (KAH-muhn-tay-turz) people who report on the action of and give opinions about an event

commissioner (kuh-MISH-uhn-ur) the person in charge of a professional sport

conferences (KAHN-fur-uhns-iz) associations of athletic teams

continental (kahn-tuh-NEN-tuhl) being part of the United States on the North American continent

dynasty (DYE-nuh-stee) a group of rulers from the same family or group

league (LEEG) a group of sports teams that regularly play one another

resale price (REE-sayl PRISE) the amount that something previously paid for is being sold for again

rosters (RAH-sturz) lists of people who belong to a particular group

salaries (SAL-ur-eez) money people get for a job over a year

INDEX